P9-DCY-710

OTTO Goes to School

Todd PARR

Megan Tingley Books
LITTLE, BROWN AND COMPANY
New York Boston

To Morgan Grace
Love,
Todd

Other OTTO Adventures

OTTO Goes to Bed
OTTO Goes to the Beach
OTTO Goes to Camp
OTTO Has a Birthday Party

Little, Brown and Company

Time Warner Book Group
1271 Avenue of the Americas, New York, NY 10020
Visit our Web site at www.lb-kids.com

First Edition

Library of Congress Cataloging-in-Publication Data

Parr, Todd.
Otto goes to school / Todd Parr.—1st ed.
p. cm.
Summary: After a breakfast of juice, cereal, and a banana split, Otto goes to school for the first time, where he makes new friends and learns how to wag his tail without knocking things over.
ISBN 0-316-83533-1
[1. First day of school—Fiction. 2. Schools—Fiction. 3. Dogs—Fiction.] I. Title.
PZ7.P2447Ose 2005
[E]—dc22 2004010273

10 9 8 7 6 5 4 3 2 1

TWP

Printed in Singapore

Wake up, Otto!

It's the first day of school!

Otto gets dressed, but
he is so excited he puts
his shirt on backward
and wears two different-
color socks.

Silly Otto!

He eats his favorite breakfast—
cereal, juice, and a banana split.

"Yum!" says Otto.

"Honk! Honk!" The bus is here.
Otto gets on and rides to school.

At school, Otto sees red dogs, blue dogs, big dogs, little dogs, and even a polka-dotted cat. Otto is a little worried because he doesn't know anyone.

SCHOOL

Otto's teacher shows him to his class. Then Otto sees his friends, Cool Kitty and Noodle Poodle, and that makes him feel better.

He learns all kinds of things, like:

How to wag his tail without knocking things over.

Good dog, Otto!

That shoes are for wearing, not for eating.

How to share his toys and play games.

Good dog, Otto!

He learns it's not okay to pull the cat's tail . . .

Or to chase squirrels.

Good dog, Otto!

And he learns to wait his turn for the bathroom.

Good dog, Otto!

Otto loves the first day
of school. He is so good
that he gets a special
treat and a blue ribbon.

But on the way home from school, Otto rolls in a puddle and tracks mud all over the house.

Oh no, Otto!

Otto still has a few things to learn!

The first day of school is fun and exciting. You will make new friends, learn new things, and you will be really smart.

Love, Otto and Todd